John Kilaka

True Friends

A Tale from Tanzania

Groundwood Books / House of Anansi Press Toronto Berkeley

Rat was the only one who knew how to make fire. Early every morning, all the animals would crowd around and watch while Rat rubbed a special stick against a log until there was a spark. When the fire was burning, he would give some to each of his friends so that they could cook their food.

Rat liked all the animals, but Elephant was his best friend.

Elephant and Rat were next-door neighbors, but they couldn't have been more different. Rat never stopped working. He gathered and stored grain, even when the harvest was good.

But Elephant liked to sit outside his house and relax. Why work so hard when there was plenty of food for everyone?

Then one season the rains did not come. The crops in the fields began to wilt.

Elephant saw the cloudless sky and the brown earth, and he began to worry.

"I have a big stomach, and I need lots of food to fill it. That means I'll be the first to go hungry. I'd better pay my friend Rat a visit."

So Elephant went to see Rat.

"The fields are dry this season," he said.

"Yes," said Rat. "But I'm not worried. I have enough to last through the bad times."

"You do have a good supply," agreed Elephant. "But your little house is open on all sides. Aren't you worried about thieves? Why not keep your food at my place? My house has a door and sturdy walls."

Rat thought about it.

"You are my best friend," he said. "I trust you. Take the food and look after it for me. I will come and get it from you when I need it."

"Don't worry about a thing," called Elephant, as he heaved the sacks of grain onto his shoulders and hurried home.

Weeks later, when the land was dry and parched and there was not a speck of grain to be found, Rat went next door to Elephant's house.

"I have come to fetch the grain you have been keeping for me," he said.

But he was in for a terrible shock.

"You have a tiny stomach and you don't need much. But I am big and I need lots of food," Elephant said cruelly. "Now go away and leave me alone!"

Rat could not believe his ears.

"What kind of friend would do such a thing?" he cried. And he decided to run away from the village.

The next day, the other animals came to Rat's house as usual to fetch the fire they needed to cook their breakfast. But Rat was nowhere to be found.

"Do you know where Rat is?" they asked Elephant. But he just shrugged and shook his head.

"Why would he disappear like that?" said Zebra. "Could someone have driven him away? If so, they had better watch out. Rat has a secret power — the power of fire. He could come back and burn down his enemy's house."

Elephant was horrified.

"You must all stay here and help me protect my house!" he cried.

"What are you worried about?" asked Pig. "You are Rat's best friend."

Elephant hung his head in shame. "I stole Rat's food, and now I'm scared. You have to help me."

The animals backed away. "You're on your own now!" they said angrily.

So Elephant went to see Lion.

Lion is big and strong, he thought. He's not afraid of anyone. He'll help me.

But Lion shook his head and waved Elephant away.

"How can you be afraid of a tiny animal like Rat?" Elephant asked.

"It's true that I am king of the animals," said Lion, "and I fear no other creature. But I am afraid of fire. What if Rat decides to burn down my house when he finds out I have protected a thief? No, you are the one who created this mess. You will have to look after yourself."

Back at home, Elephant sat outside his house and worried. Would Rat come and set his house on fire? Would he sneak up behind him in the black of night? Was he hiding in the hills even now?

Elephant decided to climb a tree to keep watch. He waited, and watched, and waited some more.

By midnight, he could no longer keep his eyes open, and he fell fast asleep. He dreamed that Rat and his friends were chasing him with torches. Elephant could feel the heat of the flames right behind him, but he could not escape.

Elephant jerked awake. He had fallen to the ground with a heavy crash. When he tried to stand up, he felt a terrible pain in his leg.

When dawn came, Elephant limped to the hospital, where the doctors gave him a very thorough examination. They patched up his cuts and bruises, gave him a tetanus shot and wrapped a big bandage around his broken leg.

Elephant returned home, but he was all alone. His sturdy house no longer felt safe. He couldn't sleep, and his leg hurt.

Worst of all, he had lost his best friend.

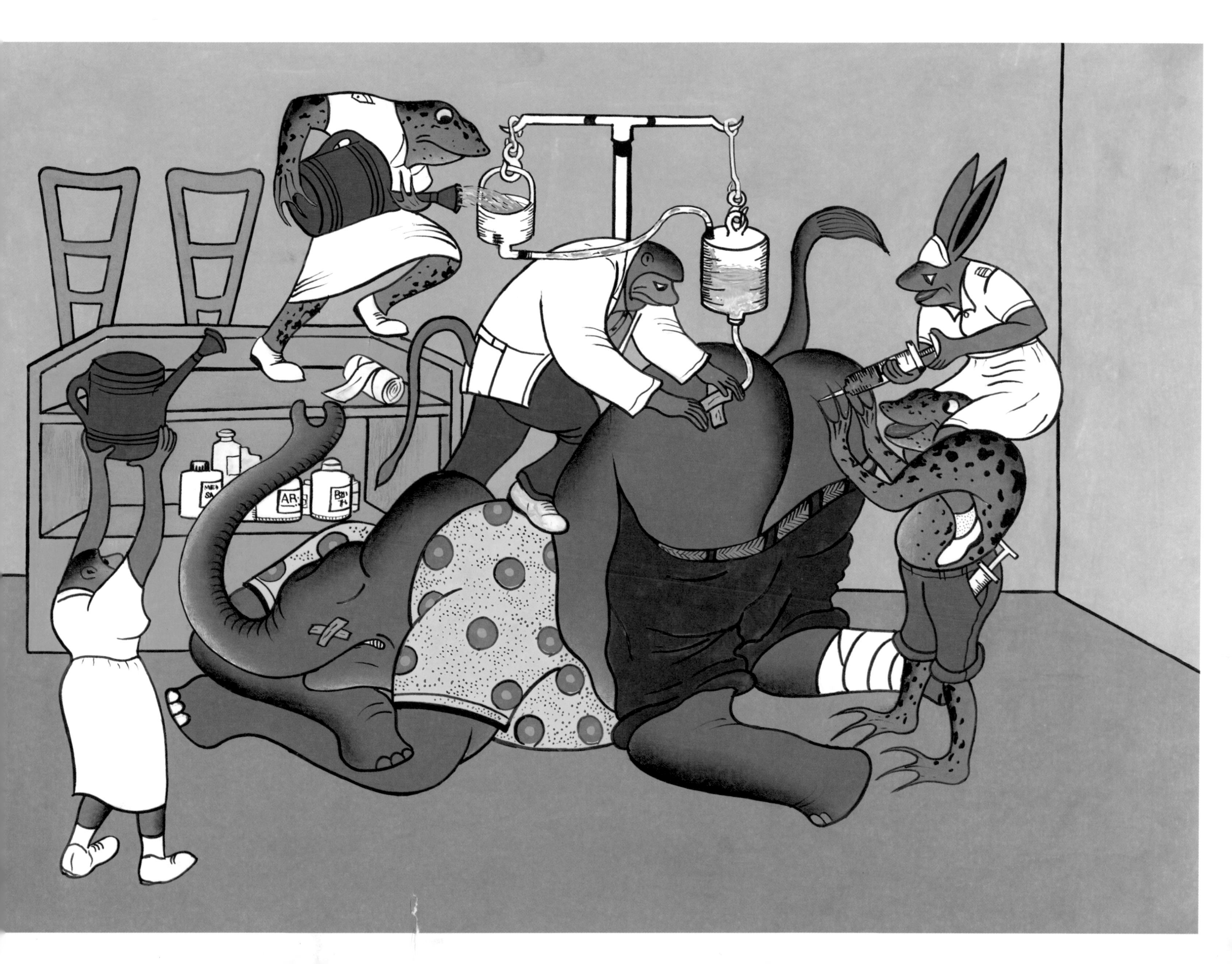

“This is no good,” he said to himself. “I have to find Rat and tell him how sorry I am, even if he is very angry with me.”

So Elephant set out to search for his friend. He looked in every cave and behind every hill. He followed every tiny set of footprints.

“Rat!” he called out again and again. But there was no answer.

In the meantime, Rat's empty stomach had got the better of him.

"I'm going to starve to death out here anyway, and I'm all alone," he said. And he set off for home.

The other animals were thrilled to see him.

"It's Rat!" they shouted. "Now we will have fire again!" And they all ran to greet him.

"But where is Elephant?" Rat asked.

The others explained that Elephant had left the village, and no one was guarding his house.

So Rat simply went in and took back his sacks of grain.

Weeks later, a tired and hungry Elephant limped into the village. He had been wandering over the countryside all this time, searching for his friend.

"Rat came home long ago, and he has taken back his sacks of grain," Frog told Elephant.

Elephant gathered up his courage and went to find his friend.

"I'm very sorry for what I did," he said. "I was wrong. I hope you can forgive me."

Rat looked Elephant straight in the eye.

"True friends don't think only of themselves, even when times are hard," he told him.

Elephant nodded.

"I know that now," he said.

So Rat forgave him. And all the animals joined them in celebrating, happy that things had been set right in their world once again.

First published in English in 2006 by Groundwood Books by arrangement with Baobab
English translation and adaptation by Shelley Tanaka

Groundwood Books / House of Anansi Press
110 Spadina Avenue, Suite 801, Toronto, Ontario M5V 2K4
Distributed in the USA by Publishers Group West
1700 Fourth Street, Berkeley, CA 94710

Library and Archives Canada Cataloguing in Publication
Kilaka, John
True Friends / John Kilaka.
Translation of: Gute freunde.
ISBN-13: 978-0-88899-698-5
ISBN-10: 0-88899-698-5
I. Title.
PZ7.K54Tr 2005 j823'.92 C2005-905118-3

Printed and bound in China